by Sarah Hines
Stephens

MONKEY MADNESS

illustrated by
Art Baltazar

Superman created by
Jerry Siegel and Joe Shuster
by special arrangement with the Jerry Siegel family

raintree
a Capstone company — publishers for children

CONTENTS

FORTRESS of SOLITUDE
SUPER-COMPUTER

SUPER-PET HERO FILE 003:
BEPPO

heat vision

X-ray vision

super-hearing

super-strong tail

flight

super-breath

S-shield

SUPERMAN

Species: Super-Monkey

Place of birth: Krypton

Age: unknown

Favourite food: chocolate-covered bananas

Bio: Moments before Krypton exploded, Superman escaped on board a tiny rocket ship. He was not alone! Beppo hitched a ride as well. On Earth, the Super-Monkey has the same powers as the Man of Steel.

Chapter 1

THE SHOW STOPPER

"Look! Up in the sky!" said a kid

entering the grounds of Bazooka's

Carnival. He pointed into the air.

The child had not seen a bird or a

plane. It was **Beppo the Super-Monkey!**

He was on the Ferris wheel. He was

enjoying a chocolate-covered banana.

A crowd stood below the animal. Everyone wanted a closer look at the monkey in the cape. They wanted to know how he had climbed up so high!

Beppo did not understand the fuss. He did not mind the attention, either. He was having too much fun.

From the Ferris wheel, Beppo could see the whole carnival. He saw animals, rides, and games. He was choosing which to enjoy first.

Suddenly, he heard screaming!

WOOOOSH!

In a flash, Beppo flew towards the cries. The noises were coming from the animal sideshow. The Super-Monkey flew closer. Terrible growls, yells, and howls joined the screams.

Beppo did not need super-vision to spot the trouble. The problem was huge! The evil ape, **Gorilla Grodd**, was ripping apart animal cages. He was freeing the wild beasts!

"Be free!" Grodd shouted.

Crocodiles, bears, and zebras were running through the crowd. It looked like the lion was next!

Beppo shook his head. The big cat looked almost as frightened as the crowd of people.

Beppo did not like to see animals in cages. But setting wild animals loose in a city was a recipe for trouble. It put everyone in danger, including the animals.

Beppo knew Grodd. The gorilla would rather fight humans than free animals. Swinging into action, Beppo shouted at Grodd to stop his monkey business.

Grodd froze. Then he slowly turned. He looked at the little monkey. His eyes became red. The evil ape spotted the large "S" on Beppo's uniform. It was just like the one his enemy, Superman, wore on his chest.

Grodd beat his own chest with his fists.

BAM! BAM! BAM!

"You think you can stop me,

Super-Pet?" Grodd shouted.

Beppo the Super-Monkey did not

mind being called a pet. He was proud

of the S-shield on his uniform. He was

a mighty super hero!

Yes, Beppo thought. *I can stop Grodd.*

I will protect these people.

GROOARR!

With a roar, Grodd pulled another

bar from the lion cage. The crazy cat

leapt out! The crowd hurried to get

away from the wild beast and the

giant ape.

"Help! Save us!" yelled the crowd.

Beppo flew to the front of the mob.

He had to stop the madness. The

people parted around him.

Circus animals and scared people ran in all directions. Beppo needed to sort them out. He had to get the animals away from the people. They needed to go back in their cages.

But how?

Chapter 2

LET THE GAMES BEGIN

Suddenly, **the Wonder Twins, Zan and Jayna,** appeared beside Beppo. They had come to see the carnival. Like all heroes, they came running when they heard cries for help.

Beppo was happy to see his friends, especially their monkey, **Gleek**.

"Need a hand?" Jayna asked. She

bumped fists with her brother.

"WONDER TWIN POWERS ACTIVATE!"

the twins shouted into the air.

"Form of ... an ice pen!" Zan said.

"Shape of ... a sheep dog!" Jayna

said in return. The twins transformed.

In their new forms, they started

herding the frightened

animals into the pen.

Gleek headed for the gate. Beppo called out to the blue monkey. "Let them handle the animals," he said. "We've got bigger problems!" The Super-Monkey pointed at Grodd.

The super-sized ape was holding a candyfloss machine up in the air. He had eaten all the pink fluff out of it. Grodd was about to toss the metal box into a crowd.

Grodd saw Beppo looking. He threw the machine over his shoulder with a laugh. HAHAHA!

WOOSH!

Beppo flew to the rescue! The Super-Monkey caught the heavy machine before it could hurt anyone.

candyfloss

"Who let you off your leash?"

shouted Grodd. Then he saw Gleek.

His lip curled in anger. **"You brought**

a friend? Now there are two of

you trained fools?"

Beppo the Super-Monkey was not

about to be teased. He was not about

to let Grodd catch on to the Wonder

Twins' plan either.

"Strength isn't everything," Beppo

told the ape. **"It's time we cut you**

down to size."

"Are you challenging me?" Grodd asked. He let out an evil laugh.

HAHAHAHA!

It was a scary sound. But Beppo and Gleek were not frightened.

"Yes," Beppo said. He looked around and thought fast. **"We're challenging you … to a marvellous monkey duel."**

The Super-Monkey pointed at the carnival game booths. Gleek's eyebrows shot up with surprise.

"You think you can beat me at some silly human stuff?" Grodd wondered aloud. "The only thing stupider than working for humans is playing their simple games. This should be easy!" The gorilla crossed his strong arms.

"But you have to play fair," Beppo said, laying down the ground rules. **"No mind games!"**

Grodd had the power to control other people's thoughts. He could move things with his mind. Getting the villain to play fair would not be easy.

"Crushing you will be no problem,"
Grodd said. "Why don't you go first?"

A colourful board of balloons hung
at the back of the first game booth.
Beppo picked up an armful of darts.
He threw them at the board.

The Super-Monkey popped them all.

Gleek put more balloons up on the board. Beppo stepped back to give Grodd a shot. The gorilla picked up a giant dart. He aimed and threw.

SMAAAASH!

His first dart sailed all the way through the board. It buried itself in the dirt. When the giant darts had all been thrown, three balloons still hung on the board.

"He cheated!" Grodd shouted. The evil ape believed Gleek had made the game harder to win.

Gleek shook his head. Beppo quickly soared over to the next game.

WOOOSH!

The ring toss was one of Beppo's favourite games. He had just the right touch. Every ring he threw circled the top of a milk bottle.

FWIP! FWIP! FWIP!

If they were playing for prizes, he would have won a soft toy as big as Grodd!

On the other hand, the evil ape could not even hit the milk bottles. Without his mind powers, he was just an overgrown gorilla!

Gleek snickered.

It was hard enough for Grodd to lose at human games. Being laughed at by a space monkey was the last straw. His eyes turned red. His anger took over.

The giant gorilla smashed the game booths as if they were made of cardboard. Milk bottles flew. Prizes spilled on to the grass.

With evil in his eye, Grodd turned on Beppo and Gleek. "I was wrong about you two. You're worse than silly pets in your little outfits," Grodd shouted. **"You're clowns!"**

Using his mind powers, the villain carried Beppo and Gleek through the air. He threw them in a cage.

He locked the metal prison shut with his mind. **SLAM!**

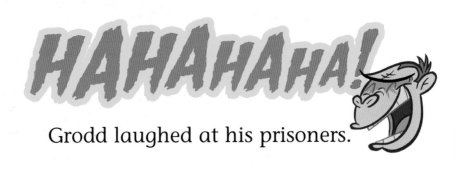

HAHAHAHA!

Grodd laughed at his prisoners.

Gleek screamed in fright. He had been a carnival animal before. Long ago on the planet Exxor, he had performed under the big top. Zan and Jayna had been there, too.

Just the memory of those days made Gleek shiver. The little blue monkey sat in the corner of the cage, helpless.

Chapter 3

BRINGING DOWN THE HOUSE

Luckily, no cage could hold Beppo.

As long as humans and animals

were in danger, nothing could stop

him. Using his heat vision, the

Super-Monkey melted the steel bars.

ZRRRRRT!

Pulling Gleek along, Beppo flew after Grodd. The monster had finally seen the Wonder Twins' plan.

All the circus animals had been rounded up by Jayna in her sheep dog form. The beasts were safely contained in Zan's ice pen.

On the other side of the fence, people stumbled around in fear. Grodd walked over to them with angry eyes.

The gorilla giant towered high over the helpless crowd. ROAR!

The only things even close to the giant ape's size were the circus elephants. These beasts had helped raise up the huge big top.

That gave Beppo an idea.

Freed from the cage, Gleek was ready to help. The first thing they needed to do was to get Grodd to look at them.

WHHIRRRRRRRL

Gleek's tail began to spin like a helicopter. He lifted off. He headed over to the snack stand.

In a flash, Beppo and Gleek were
back and armed. They swooped
around Grodd's head. At the same
time, they threw chicken drumsticks,
hot dogs, and ice cream cones at the
angry ape. SPLAT!

The villain swung at them. He missed each time. Gleek and Beppo dodged, dipped, and threw a few handfuls of chips.

WHAP! SPLAT!

Covered in food, Grodd opened his mouth to roar. His timing was perfect. At that moment, Beppo launched a pint of soft serve ice cream at the target. Gleek topped it off with a cherry. Bull's-eye!

SPA-LOOP!

Before Grodd could move, the monkeys headed over to the big top.

Wiping sticky vanilla goo from his eyes, Grodd followed. Beppo had hoped that would happen.

The Super-Monkey flew into the tent
with the giant gorilla on his heels.
Grabbing the trapeze artists' net, he
stretched it across the doorway. Grodd
walked right into Beppo's web. The ape
got twisted in the net.

Outside, Gleek worked as fast as he could. He loosened the ropes that held up the big top.

In the tent, Beppo loaded the clown's cannon with popcorn. He fired! The popcorn blinded Grodd. He roared and swung his fists in Beppo's direction.

Beppo was ready. He was flying near one of the giant poles that held the tent up.  POW! Grodd was powerful, but Beppo was fast. Beppo dodged and Grodd missed again. SMASH! And again.

Beppo smiled. Grodd's misses were just what the super hero wanted. Each time the ape smashed another pole, the tent swayed a little more.

Finally, Beppo ducked out of the tent. He took to the sky. **WOOSH!**

The Super-Monkey told Gleek to make sure all the people were standing clear. Jayna helped. She guided everyone to safety with her barks.

The grunts and roars from inside the tent sent chills down Beppo's spine. His plan was working. The ropes that had held the tent up were ripping loose, thanks to Gleek.

It was time to bring down the house!

Beppo took off. He picked up speed. Faster and faster Beppo flew around the brightly coloured tent. He created a tornado of air.

WOOOSH!

The force of the wind spun around Grodd like a cocoon. It wrapped him tight in the heavy tent.

The crowd cheered. The strongman lifted Gleek and Beppo on to his shoulders. The elephants trumpeted loudly to their heroes.

Even the ringmaster came over to thank Beppo and Gleek. "The show must go on," he said.

"Hip, hip, hooray!" the crowd shouted together.

Beppo loved the carnival. It was his favourite place! But now, the carnival was even better since he could enjoy it with his friends.

And Grodd – the carnival's Big Top Banana – was a sideshow smash!

THE END

Krypto

Streaky

Beppo

Comet

Ace

Jumpa

Whatzit

B'dg

Storm

Topo

Ark

Hoppy

Paw Pooch

Bull Dog

Chameleon Collie

Hot Dog

These are **HERO PETS.**

Tail Terrier

Tusky Husky

SUPER-PETS

 Ignatius

 Chauncey

 Crackers

 Giggles

 Artie Puffin

 Griff

 Waddles

 Rozz

 Dex-Starr

 Glomulus

 Misty

 Sneezers

 Whoosh

 Pronto

 Snorrt

 Rolf

 Squealer

 Kajunn

These are **VILLAIN PETS.**

JOKES

Hey, Beppo! What's a monkey's favourite cookie?

What?

Chocolate chimp!

What do you get when two monkeys fight over a banana?

Beats me.

A banana split!

What side of a monkey has more hair?

I don't know.

The OUTside!

GLOSSARY

activate to turn on or cause to work

big top main tent at a circus or carnival, where performances are held

cocoon protective case used by some baby insects

ringmaster person in charge of performances at a circus or carnival

sideshow small show in addition to the main attraction at a circus, carnival, or fair

trapeze bar hanging from two ropes, which circus performers use to swing through the air

uniform special set of clothes worn by a specific group, such as super heroes

Word Powers ... **ACTIVATE!**

53

MEET THE AUTHOR

Sarah Hines Stephens

Sarah Hines Stephens has written more than 60 books for children about all kinds of characters, from Jedi to princesses. When she is not writing, gardening, or saving the world by teaching people about recycling, Sarah enjoys spending time with her heroic husband, two kids, and super friends.

MEET THE ILLUSTRATOR

Eisner Award-winner Art Baltazar

Art Baltazar defines cartoons and comics not only as a style of art, but as a way of life. Art is the creative force behind *The New York Times* best-selling, Eisner Award-winning, DC Comics series Tiny Titans and the co-writer for *Billy Batson and the Magic of SHAZAM!* Art draws comics and never has to leave the house. He lives with his lovely wife, Rose, big boy Sonny, little boy Gordon, and little girl Audrey.

Art Baltazar says:

Read all the DC SUPER-PETS stories today!

Raintree is an imprint of Capstone Global Library Limited, a company incorporated in England and Wales having its registered office at 264 Banbury Road, Oxford, OX2 7DY – Registered company number: 6695582

www.raintree.co.uk
myorders@raintree.co.uk

First published by Picture Window Books in 2011
First published in the United Kingdom in 2012
The moral rights of the proprietor have been asserted.

STAR26250

Art Director and Designer: Bob Lentz
Editors: Donald Lemke and Vaarunika Dharmapala
Production Specialist: Michelle Biedscheid
Creative Director: Heather Kindseth
Editorial Director: Michael Dahl

ISBN 978 1 4747 6442 1 (paperback)
21 20 19 18 17
10 9 8 7 6 5 4 3 2 1

British Library Cataloguing in Publication Data
A full catalogue record for this book is available from the British Library.

Printed and bound in India